PUFFIN BOOKS
HAVE YOU MET THE PARSIS?

Anastasia Damani is an illustrator-turned-author, musician and theatre lover. When she's not donning one of these hats, she likes curling up with a warm cup of tea. After completing her graduation from Symbiosis Institute of Design, Pune with a degree in communication design, she began her journey in her hometown, Kolkata, and now lives in København (Copenhagen). Anastasia enjoys writing and illustrating across mediums with children's books as her first love. Through her work, she strives to promote love, confidence, respect and responsibility in children.

ADVANCE PRAISE FOR THE BOOK

'What a cutely original introduction to a community that is minuscule in number, big of heart and remarkable in achievement. Parsi by marriage, Anastasia brings an outsider's objectivity, an insider's warmth, presenting a feast of information made easily digestible with charming illustrations'—Bachi Karkaria, columnist and author

For
Silloo Granny and Jamshed Grandpa,
Shireen Granny and Bomi Grandpa

Have you met THE PARSIS?

(Culture • Customs • Community)

written + illustrated by
Anastasia Damani

PUFFIN BOOKS

An imprint of Penguin Random House

PUFFIN BOOKS

USA | Canada | UK | Ireland | Australia
New Zealand | India | South Africa | China | Singapore

Puffin Books is part of the Penguin Random House group of companies
whose addresses can be found at global.penguinrandomhouse.com

Published by Penguin Random House India Pvt. Ltd
4th Floor, Capital Tower 1, MG Road,
Gurugram 122 002, Haryana, India

First published in Puffin Books by Penguin Random House India 2021

Text and illustrations copyright © Anastasia Damani 2021

ISBN 9780143451440

Typeset in Montserrat
Printed at Thomson Press India Ltd, New Delhi

introduction

Meeting new people can be exciting! Especially people who are different from us. This helps us open our hearts and minds to new cultures.

My first interaction with the Parsis was with my then school friend and now husband. Being a part of his family opened up a whole new world for me that I knew so little about.

Respect and appreciation for the diversity in communities, food, language, religion and attire does not necessarily come naturally. Taking the time to broaden our horizons ensures that we not only **learn about** these differences but also **learn to love** them.

The best way to do this is to make new friends—it could be a neighbour, a classmate or perhaps even a character in a book.

Meet Uncle Cyrus and
Aunty Jeroo Theatrewala.
They have three children: big
brother Darius and twin sisters
Farah and Freya. The sixth
member of the family
is Twiggy Theatrewala,
the dachshund.

The Theatrewalas are
parsis.

The word 'Parsi' means 'Persian' in *avestan*, which is an ancient Persian language. Hundreds of years ago, the people who lived in Persia had to flee their homeland because it was not safe for them to live there any more.

So the Parsis gathered what they could and travelled to India by sea in the hope of building new lives. Today, the country of Persia is known as Iran and the language they speak is Farsi.

A fascinating story in Parsi folklore tells us that the Parsis sailed to India on large wooden boats and landed in a town called Sanjan in Gujarat.

2

The king of Sanjan sent the people of Persia a vessel of milk filled to the brim to show them that just like the vessel, the land was full and there was no room for more people. The Parsis responded by adding a pinch of sugar in the milk. The vessel did not overflow, but the milk got a little sweeter. This simple act made the king realize that the Parsis would be able to blend in peacefully with the people of Gujarat and do their part to make the land better. Highly impressed by this, the king welcomed the Parsis in his kingdom.

The Parsis sailed from **Hormuz** in Persia to **Sanjan** in Gujarat.

Let's do a fun activity. Grab a world map and a white sheet of paper. Spot and trace modern-day Persia and the state of Gujarat from the map on to your sheet. You could also trace some of the neighbouring states and countries between these two places.

Now draw the route that you think the Parsis might have taken. How many boats do you think they used to make their journey? Draw those along the route that you have marked out.

(asti) ← (vahishtem) ← (vohu) ← (ashem)

(ahmai) ← (ushta) ← (asti) ← (ushta)

(ashem) ← (vahishtai) ← (ashai) ← (hyat)

You're probably used to writing and reading from left to right, but Avestan is written and read from right to left. Unfortunately, this is an extinct language now as the Parsis learnt to communicate in Gujarati when they settled in India. They did this so that they could blend in as promised. Like sugar in milk, remember?

ashem vohu prayer

(don't forget to read it →
(way ← ← this

The Parsis have worked hard to preserve the oral recitation of the prayers, sacred texts and scriptures, but over the years, these have evolved to include a mix of Avestan and Farsi. Most sacred scripts are now written completely in Gujarati, including the *Avesta*, the holy book of the Parsis.

યયા અહૂ વઇથ્યો આયા
રતુશ આષાત યીત હચા
વધ્હેઉરા હજ઼ા મનંધહો
નાંમ આધહેઉરા મઝ઼દાઇ
ક્ષથ્રેમયા અહઉરાઇ આ યિમ
દ્રેગુબ્યો હહત વાસ્તારેમ

Like most Parsis, Uncle Cyrus and Aunty Jeroo can speak both Gujarati and English, but their Gujarati has a little twist. When they talk and laugh, others seldom know what they're saying. It's almost like a Parsi conversation code!

Try using these Parsi words in your next conversation with your friends. It'll be fun!

mba

Mane Baddha Avech (I know everything; a know-it-all)

'Xerxes never stops talking. He has an MBA in everything!'

bhoot nu bharoso

As reliable as a ghost

'You can never tell if Jal is going to show up or not. With him, it is always bhoot nu bharoso.'

photo frame thai gyu

When someone passes away and becomes a photo frame

'Nilufer's plants photo frame thai gyu because she always forgets to water them.'

aafat par eeda

Problems with eggs on top; too many problems

———————

'I lost the football match and tore my shoe right after. Such aafat par eeda!'

dhoom dhuss ne keri chuss

When it all falls apart, sit back and enjoy a mango.

———————

'Your twisted ankle will heal soon. For now, dhoom dhuss ne keri chuss.'

kasari nu kaan

Ears like a cockroach; extremely sharp hearing

———————

'Don't discuss anything important right now, Aunty Dinaz is close by and has kasari nu kaan.'

dikra, dikri, it's bhonu time!

'Dikra' and 'dikri' is what you call a younger boy and girl respectively. 'Bhonu' means food.

The Theatrewalas live in Khorshed Madan Mansion in Kolkata. Several Parsi families live together in this mansion as a community. In the evenings, some grown-ups chat and play cards. The children run around and have fun while their parents ensure that they're safe and happy. Many Parsis all over India live together in buildings or complexes like this. These are known as baugs.

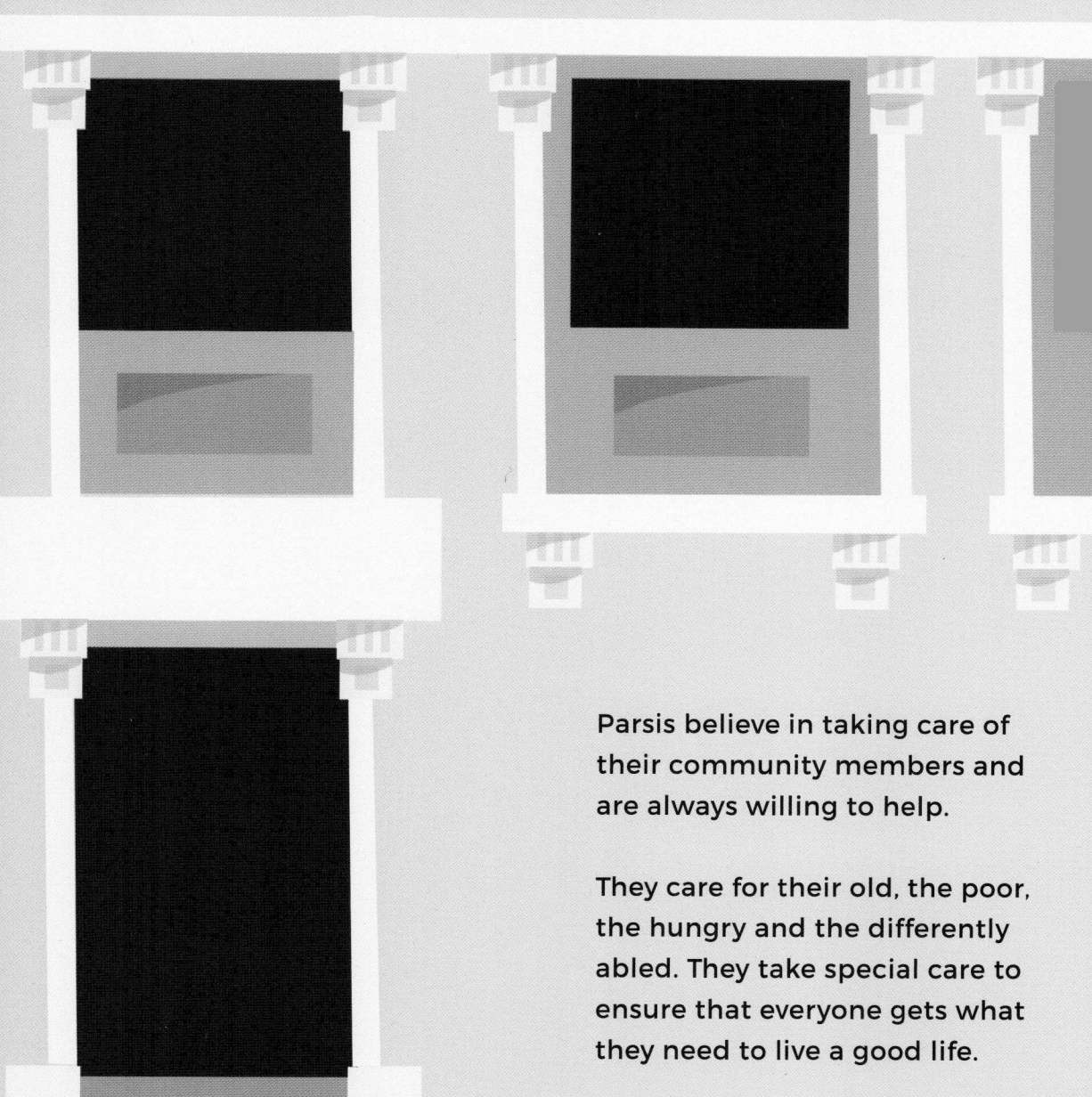

Parsis believe in taking care of their community members and are always willing to help.

They care for their old, the poor, the hungry and the differently abled. They take special care to ensure that everyone gets what they need to live a good life.

The Parsis worship their God, Ahura Mazda, through a sacred fire that burns continuously. When they sailed to India from Persia, they brought their sacred fire with them and have kept it burning ever since. The Parsi religion is called Zoroastrianism, named after Prophet Zarathustra.

asho farohar

The Zoroastrian place of worship is a fire temple, which is known as an agyari. Uncle Cyrus, Aunty Jeroo, Farah, Freya and Darius go to the fire temple to offer prayers on special occasions.

ses items

humata, hukhta, hvarshta

means 'good thoughts, good words and good deeds' in Avestan. This is an important Zoroastrian belief.

Every Parsi household has a ses, consisting of various items, which is used on auspicious occasions. The Asho Farohar is a Parsi symbol that can be found on a Parsi's car, front door, cupboard or even jewellery. It is like their guardian angel. Aunty Jeroo made an Asho Farohar locket necklace for each of her children to wear around their necks.

PS: Did you know that the name and logo of the global automobile company Mazda are inspired by Ahura Mazda and the wings of the Asho Farohar?

Last year, Darius had his navjote, a ceremony by which a Parsi child adopts the Zoroastrian faith. A Parsi priest performs the ritual.

Darius wore a topi—a ceremonial cap—as the priest led him through his prayers. He did this while tying his kushti around his sedreh. A sedreh is a sacred vest that is worn by a Parsi at all times, and a kushti is a cord made from lamb's wool that is wrapped around the sedreh thrice. This is done while reciting three short prayers in Avestan.

pocket of good deeds

↓

The sedreh features a symbolic pocket known as the 'pocket of good deeds'. It's meant for collecting and storing all the good deeds you do during the day. Darius is excited about filling his special pocket.

How many good deeds can you collect in a day? Write them down in your very own 'pocket of good deeds' right here.

·THEATREWALAS·

The Parsis celebrate navroz, which is their new year. On Navroz morning, Uncle Cyrus hangs a string of flowers known as a toran above their main door. Darius and Freya make a decoration with powdered chalk at the entrance.

The chalk isn't just decorative; it also keeps insects away as it is made with lime powder. A metal stencil is used to make these designs. Follow these simple instructions to make your own fish stencil and decorate a corner of your house.

materials

15-inch-long aluminium foil
1 kitchen sponge
1 kebab skewer
Some talcum powder

instructions

1 Roll in the edges of the foil to create a square. The edges should be raised, leaving a flat inner surface, like a square pizza with a crust. Then place the kitchen sponge under the foil.

2 Using the pointy end of the skewer like a pencil, lightly draw out this fish shape. Make sure to only crease the foil, making an impression. Be very careful not to tear the foil.

3 Once you have a rough outline of your fish shape, you can start poking holes along the outline. Remember to maintain a very light touch and do not make the holes too close to each other because the foil might rip.

4 When you are done, the outline should look perforated. Evenly layer the top surface of the foil with talcum powder.

5 Take it off the sponge. Find a dark surface to make your design on. Now gently drop the stencil on the floor from a height of 2 inches off the ground.

done!!

Rotate your stencil and create multiple impressions to form a pattern. You could make a fishy somersault pattern like this one!

After the house is decorated, the Theatrewalas go to the agyari to pray for the new year. Before entering the prayer hall, they wash their hands with water from a well, untie the kushti and retie it around the waist. In the prayer hall, they light *divos* (oil lamps) and offer sandalwood pieces to keep the sacred fire burning.

Later in the day, Uncle Cyrus, Aunty Jeroo and the kids go to greet all their relatives. They take with them fish-shaped sweetmeats. The fish is a popular symbol of good luck for the Parsis.

Khordad Saal, celebrated as Prophet Zarathustra's birthday, is another important Zoroastrian festival along with Ava Roj, Ava Mahino (a tribute to the angel of water) and Adar Roj, Adar Mahino (a tribute to the angel of fire).

Twiggy Theatrewala's favourite time of the day is bhonu time!

On special occasions like Navroz, birthdays and anniversaries, Uncle Cyrus and Aunty Jeroo prepare Parsi bhonu like dhandar, fish patio and salli boti. Twiggy Theatrewala loves all of them!

Some more popular Parsi recipes are prawn patio, patra-ni-macchi, lagan-nu-stew, dhansak, ravo and lagan-nu-custard.

salli boti

dhansak

ravo

prawn patio

lagan-nu-custard

papeta par eeda

Parsis are especially fond of eggs. Many of their dishes have a fried or beaten egg on top. The Parsi term for egg is 'eeda'. So a typical egg dish has the terms 'par eeda' in it, meaning 'eggs on top'. Papeta (potato) par eeda, tamota (tomato) par eeda, bheeda (okra) par eeda are some examples.

What would you put an egg on top of and turn into an interesting dish? A roti, toast or khichdi? Write your recipe ideas below.

_____

_____

_____

_____

_____

doodh-na-puff

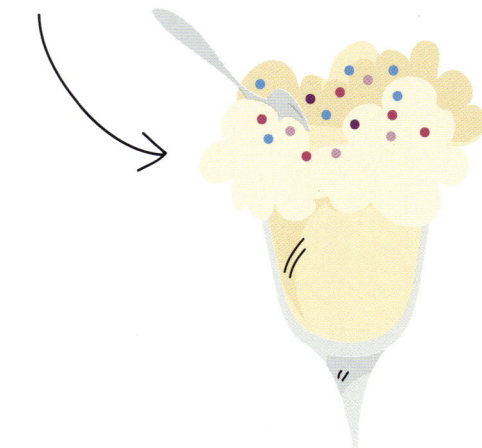

Easy to make, this is a sweet cloud of milk froth in a glass! Freya, Farah and Darius love having it. Not to be left behind, Twiggy Theatrewala licks the glasses after they're done.

ingredients

2 cups full-fat milk
3–4 tbsp sugar
Any sprinkles (the more colourful, the better)

preparation

1 **Ask an adult** to bring the milk to a boil in a saucepan.

2 After the milk has been taken off the stove, **you can** stir in the sugar. Keep stirring the milk gently so that a layer of cream does not form as the milk cools down.

3 Once the milk reaches room temperature, **you can** keep it in the fridge overnight.

4 The next day, **ask an adult** to help you whisk the milk with an electric whisk. Watch as soft, puffy milk clouds start to form. **You can** scoop up the foam and transfer it to a glass.

5 Once the glass is full to the brim with the foam, **you can** add the colourful sprinkles on top.

ta-da!

Scoop up the puff with your spoon and imagine that you're floating on a cloud!

Here's a tasty recipe of scrambled eggs or paneer with green garlic. It's a breakfast special in the Theatrewalas household.

Leela-Lasan-ni-Akuri

ingredients

2 eggs, or a small chunk of paneer or tofu
2–3 sprigs of green garlic leaves or chives
1–2 sprigs of coriander
½ green chilli (if desired)
A pinch of salt
2 tbsp oil

preparation

1. **You can** snip the green garlic, coriander and green chilli (if using) into a bowl with a pair of kitchen scissors.

2) **Ask an adult** to crack the eggs into the bowl for you. If opting for the eggless version, **you can** crumble the paneer. Add salt and whisk whisk whisk.

3) Now **ask an adult** to heat some oil in a pan and pour in the egg or paneer mixture.

4) **You can, with the help of an adult**, stir the mixture and scramble the eggs or paneer.

5) **Ask an adult** to turn off the heat once the akuri is cooked. It should be mushy and not too dry.

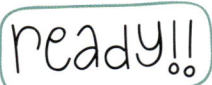

ready!!

Turn it on to a plate and devour your lip-smacking leela-lasan-ni-akuri with a slice of toast or roti.

Farah and Freya are excited to attend their first Parsi wedding. Their neighbour is getting married in the Parsi month of Adar.

Usually, the bride dresses in a delicate white lace or embroidered saree draped in a Parsi style. This is similar to the Gujarati way of wearing a saree, except the pallu hangs lower and more triangular.

The groom wears white trousers and a white overcoat called a dugli. The overcoat is wrapped and tied with two bows down the centre. He also wears a formal headgear known as a pheta.

Just like the navjote, a priest conducts the wedding ceremony. It takes place at the exact moment the sun sets in the evening. Can you imagine what a storybook setting that would make?

Have you ever been to a Parsi wedding? It is made up of many meaningful rituals. Farah and Freya can't wait to be a part of all of them. Here are some customs that the Theatrewala twins are looking forward to.

madasaro

This ritual involves planting a fruit tree. It is performed four days before the wedding and marks the beginning of the celebrations. The bride and groom's families each plant a sapling of a fruit tree in a decorated pot. The little tree-to-be is kept outside each family home and is watered every morning. After the wedding, it is moved to a permanent outdoor home. The plant is like a couple's life together—if the sapling is given water and sunshine, it will grow into a big fruit tree.

rice race

In this ritual, which is called the Ara Antar, the bride and groom sit opposite each other with a curtain separating them. After the ceremony is completed, the curtain is lowered and the bride and groom are asked to shower each other with handfuls of raw rice. They both move quickly to be the first to toss the rice at each other.

It's good to be the first to do some things in life, like to show kindness, generosity or to ask for forgiveness when you're wrong.

Similarly, if the bride and groom grow in love and friendship, they will have a happy home.

Most families prefer to plant a mango tree. What would you choose?

The Theatrewalas are all set. Uncle Cyrus and Darius dress up in duglis, Aunty Jeroo wears a beautifully embroidered saree called a *gara* and the girls look pretty in pink and purple dresses with matching embroidery called *jhablas*.

One of the traditional embroidery patterns is referred to as the china-chini because Chinese master craftsmen hand embroidered these.

Often weaved into the designs were scenes from China, depicting Chinese girls and boys.

These embroidery stitches are very minute and delicate, and one of them is the Pekinese stitch. It came to be known as the forbidden stitch because rumour has it that the craftsmen would go blind upon completing the entire saree.

When a daughter would be born into a Parsi family, very often, her mother would start to hand embroider a saree border called a *kor*.

This border would then be stitched on to a beautiful saree and gifted to her on her wedding day.

This is an example of a china-chini pattern.
You can trace it on to a piece of fabric and, **with the help of an adult**, embroider it. You could even colour it in right here!

Every weekend, Farah, Freya and Darius go to the Parsi Sports Club for tennis coaching. After that, they play some ball with Twiggy Theatrewala.

The Parsis enjoy playing a lot of sports—hockey, tennis, football, table tennis, cricket, basketball and rugby, to name a few. Every year, five cities across India—Kolkata, Secunderabad, Surat, Jamshedpur and Nagpur—host a cricket tournament called a Pentangular. Farah, Freya and Darius can't wait till they're old enough to participate in it.

PARSI CLUB

Like most Parsis, Uncle Cyrus has a love for theatre and music. The whole family is part of the Calcutta Parsi Amateur Dramatic Club. Most cities in India also have a Parsi drama club that performs plays from time to time. The Parsi Navroz Natak is especially well liked. Sometimes it is even staged for the Gujarati community by popular demand.

The Parsis are a very talented community. They have excelled in a wide range of fields internationally. Here's a list of some iconic Parsis.

A journalist, columnist and renowned author, **Bachi Karkaria** has also been an editor for the *Times of India*. Truth and humour are her writing superpowers. *In Hot Blood: The Nanavati Case That Shook India* and *Dare to Dream: A Life of Rai Bahadur Mohan Singh Oberoi* are some of her bestselling books.

bachi karkaria

sam manekshaw

A field marshal is the highest military rank in the Indian army, and **Sam Manekshaw** was the first Indian army officer to be promoted to this rank. Also known as Sam Bahadur (Sam the Brave), he fought in five different wars, starting with World War II. He was awarded the Padma Vibhushan and the Padma Bhushan.

Freddie Mercury, the lead singer and songwriter of the band Queen, could sing higher and lower than most people. His vocal range spanned more than forty notes on the music scale. Most people can sing around twenty-four notes. His popular songs are 'We Will Rock You', 'I Want to Break Free' and 'Bohemian Rhapsody', which is the bestselling song of all time by a band.

freddie mercury

homai vyarawalla

India's first woman photojournalist, **Homai Vyarawalla**, fought hard to publish her photos at a time when no one would use photographs taken by a woman. She captured iconic moments in India's history, like the very first time the flag was raised in independent India.

Inspired by her mother's Parsi cooking and catering legacy, chef **Anahita Dhondy** completed the Grand Diplôme at Le Cordon Bleu London and is now the Chef-Partner at SodaBottleOpenerWala. She has been honoured with the Times Food Award and the Young Chef India award.

anahita dhondy

homi j. bhabha

Remembered as the 'father of the Indian nuclear programme', **Homi J. Bhabha** was a nuclear physicist and a professor of physics. He was nominated for the Nobel Prize for Physics and awarded the Padma Bhushan and the Adams Prize.

Television, theatre and film actor **Erick Avari** can be easily recognized from his roles in Hollywood movies like *The Mummy*, *Independence Day*, *Mr Deeds* and *Planet of the Apes*. Throughout his career, he has portrayed more than twenty-four different ethnic characters, which is proof that your identity does not define your ability.

erick avari

bhikaiji cama

How many female freedom fighters can you name? **Bhikaiji Cama** played an important role in the Indian independence movement. She was the first person to hoist an early version of the Indian flag outside of India.

After she received recognition from a well-known soap brand advertisement, **Persis Khambatta** pursued a career as a model. She won the Femina Miss India contest (1965) and went on to act in Bollywood and Hollywood movies. One of her most memorable roles was in *Star Trek* as the bald and beautiful Lieutenant Ilia.

Persis Khambatta

Jamsetji Tata

It's difficult not to come across a Tata product in our daily lives, be it a car, a tea bag or even a hospital. Regarded as the 'father of Indian industry', **Jamsetji Tata** was the founder of the Tata Group. Legend has it that he built the Taj Mahal Palace that overlooks the Gateway of India in Mumbai because he was not allowed to enter a Mumbai hotel for being an Indian.

Maestro **Zubin Mehta** is one of the world's leading music conductors. By the age of twenty-five, he had conducted the Vienna and Berlin Philharmonic Orchestras. He was also the music director of the Israel, New York and Los Angeles Philharmonic Orchestras. Besides music, he is famous for his love for red-hot chillies.

zubin mehta

dadi pudumjee

Do you like playing with puppets? That's exactly what **Dadi Pudumjee** does for a living. As designer, director, puppeteer and founder of the Ishara Puppet Theatre Trust, he works with traditional and innovative puppets across cultures. He received the Padma Shri award in 2011.

acknowledgements

A heartful of gratitude to Sohini Mitra, Arpita Nath, Aditi Batra, Antra K and the entire team at Penguin Random House India for their tireless efforts in making this book possible.

A special thank you to Mayura Misra who is truly a crusader for reading.

Last but not least, much appreciation is due to my family and friends who have cheered me on—foremost of them being my best friend and husband, Jamshed Madan.

READ MORE IN THE SERIES

Have You Met the Anglo-Indians?